THE
SEASON
THAT
NEVER WAS

THE
SEASON
THAT
NEVER WAS

LEROY WILLIS

ARCHWAY
PUBLISHING

Archway Publishing books may be ordered through booksellers or by contacting:

Archway Publishing
1663 Liberty Drive
Bloomington, IN 47403
www.archwaypublishing.com
1 (888) 242-5904

Because of the dynamic nature of the Internet, any web addresses or
links contained in this book may have changed since publication and
may no longer be valid. The views expressed in this work are solely those
of the author and do not necessarily reflect the views of the publisher,
and the publisher hereby disclaims any responsibility for them.

Any people depicted in stock imagery provided by Thinkstock are models,
and such images are being used for illustrative purposes only.
Certain stock imagery © Thinkstock.

ISBN: 978-1-4808-1895-8 (sc)
ISBN: 978-1-4808-1896-5 (e)

Library of Congress Control Number: 2015908286

Print information available on the last page.

Archway Publishing rev. date: 6/5/2015

DEDICATION

This book is dedicated to my wife Elaine, my three boys Brandyn, Dustyn, and Dobye along with the many coaches and players I worked with during my career. Also to Laura James for her tireless work in editing the original manuscript.

PREFACE

The Season That Never Was remained just that. We never had that dream season, but all the intangibles were in place as well as the hard work and planning that are equally important to be successful. So the question that might be asked is, why? And my answer is that it was not God's will. That does not mean He did not bless us. I hope and pray this book gives insight to those blessings, not in wins but in how God uses life events to build relationships that honor and glorify Him.

CHAPTER 1

Another football season has come and gone, a season full of hope and optimism ending in disappointment in that the victories were few, just one. Along with the single victory, there were nine losses. Many games offered hope that we had a chance to win even late in the game, but we lost just the same.

Once again sitting I find myself sitting here in the office with everyone finally gone except me and T. D., that's Touchdown, my dog, a big, loving, good natured Chow that just might be the best thing to come into my life except the good Lord, my wife, and my three boys. Touchdown is really not just my dog; he belongs to the football team, the kids at school, and the community. I've just been blessed to be his caretaker since someone dropped him off two years ago. It's quiet in here with all the sounds missing. It's just the smell of the field house and muddy uniforms left to remind me of another long season with time to reflect on the past ten weeks. It is a time for second guessing myself on what I could have done differently in order to have made things better. All coaches do this. It's time to think about how in spite of the nine losses that maybe we made a difference in some young lives. We showed how close a team can become each season through all that can happen in a few short weeks. It is time to just sit back on this old second-hand sofa, take a deep breath, pat Touchdown on the head, close my eyes and dream about *The Season That Never Was*.

CHAPTER 2

"Come on, fellas, get on in here and go to work. Y'all know there is nothing that comes easy. I don't know about that no pain, no gain stuff, but I do know that if we are going to improve, it has to start in the weight room. We have to get stronger and quicker and even though the Lord may not have given us much speed, we can dang well take advantage of all He gave us". That's the same old sermon these guys have heard before, most of them anyway, but it seems a little different with this group of players. It seems they are taking it a little more to their hearts. It seems as Coach Barnes puts them through our off-season work outs, that there is more hunger than before to improve. It may be just my imagination, wishful thinking, or whatever, but I'll take it.

About that time Ricky Gerber comes over and snaps me back to reality by telling me he has improved his bench press by 35 pounds during this last lift cycle that we are finishing up today before spring training starts. Ricky is really proud of his improvement under Coach Barnes's guidance during the off season. But the best part is Ricky is not the only player who has grown stronger. He is a good example of this bunch of players. He's not very big at 5' 8", 145 pounds, but, boy, does he have a big heart and the desire to get better. He will do a good job for us this year as a wide receiver. About that time Ricky gets my attention again, "hey! Coach, me and Lanny are getting a ball to go outside and throw a little."

"That's fine, Just put some sleeves on; it's cold out there."

Lanny is another good example of what players can do when they work. I told him after last season that we planned on moving him to quarterback this year, and he has really gone to work trying to get prepared. Coach Barry Snow, who coordinates our defense along with coaching the offensive line, came in about that time from checking out the baseball field snapping me back to the present again. Barry, who also coaches our baseball team, asks if I think it's good for Ricky and Lanny to be outside since it's so cold.

"I believe it will be okay as long as they wear sleeves. Anyway, it's been hard keeping them inside. They have been really excited about the spring."

About that time Coach Barnes walks up and remarks, "You know, I believe this group of guys has a little something extra. They sure have been a fun bunch to work with this off season."

Coach Snow began talking positions when the last member of our coaching staff, Coach David Meyers, walked in from the main office muttering about a student being moved into his class from another period when his room is already overcrowded. Just as the last group is finishing their workout, our talk turned to spring training, which is now only a week away. Coach Meyers started off our conversation by saying, "I'm looking forward to the changes we are making in our offense."

Then Barry chipped in, "I believe we are going to be happy with how the changes we are making will fit our players' abilities." He went on to say it was going to be fun for the players and coaches alike.

Coach Barnes remarked in his philosophical tone, "Heck, if it can't be anything else, it can be fun."

All they were saying just made me feel that much better about the coming year." You know," I said, "the best part about all we have been talking about is these guys' attitudes. I'm just tickled to death with that."

Coach Barnes followed that up by saying, "You know, if we keep talking long enough, we may decide that we can be pretty good." With that we all started getting ready to leave for the day, one day closer to spring practice.

CHAPTER 3

The day we have been waiting for since the last whistle of last season has arrived. Spring football starts today, and the weather has taken a turn for the better. The cold, damp stuff has moved out, and we have a great day to get started. Bright sunshine seems to go with football practice starting. The players are all suited up except those coming out of basketball which ended the previous Saturday night. Our Piney Grove Eagles team lost a narrow two-point heartbreaker in the final of the area tournament to Crestview. I couldn't be any more proud of the team and Coach Al Spangler though. They had played really hard and gave everything they had on the floor. Coach Spangler and I really get along well. He's really supportive of our football program, and I try to do whatever I can to help the basketball team, too. This year we had four guys that played on the basketball team, and they have until Wednesday to report for practice. Most of the athletes at Piney Grove play multiple sports, so we try our best to let them catch a breath between seasons whenever possible.

"Coach," I heard a familiar voice behind me say.

I turned around and there stood Tim Burger. He started to

say something when I interrupted him. "I thought y'all would take a couple of days off just being out of round ball. You can wait until Wednesday to join us."

Tim responded, "We all want to get started with the rest of the team. " About that time Gary, Donnie, and Billy walked up behind him shaking their heads in agreement.

"That's good." I said. "All your gear is already in your locker. Get dressed." That really said a lot for those guys, just another sign of something special going on with this bunch.

As the last player pulled his shoulder pads in place and began to adjust them, I whistled the guys to the middle of the dressing room where they all took a knee. This was how we began each practice. During this time we talked about what was on the practice schedule for the day, any problems or information that needed to be discussed, and we closed with a team prayer.

CHAPTER 4

With the first day of spring finished I couldn't be much happier with a group of youngsters. It may have been the first day with several more to go, but for the coaching staff, managers, and especially the players, this had been a special day. There was so much energy and enthusiasm. Heck, I told the team afterwards as we got together before we went in, "I'm ready to play now. Bring on them Bears." That might be a little overly optimistic, but it was sure fun out there today.

Seemed like every day just got better as the spring went on, and now we are on our last day before our annual intra-squad game, and the kids haven't let up. I know in my years around this game I have never seen a group of players who are so tuned in and coaches working and teaching from the first minute of practice until the last. They all know this has been something special without being told. Everything has just fallen into place with our new spread offense, our moving some players to different positions, and the junior high guys moving up to the varsity. I kind of feel like a kid in a candy store. I'm just beside myself with this team.

As the few seconds of the spring game ticked away with our

blue squad on top 16-14, there is really a lot of excitement among our players, coaches, and the 200 or so fans that showed up for the game. That doesn't seem like many folks, but for an intrasquad game that's very good. Even though most of them are students or parents, it's good to know that many people came out to support. It also shows our players are taking the news of our good spring home with them.

CHAPTER 5

With all the good you just know that eventually there's going to be some obstacles to overcome. As with anything, if it wasn't for the tough times, then the good would never be as appreciated. The bad in this case happened in a two-day period right before final exams. On Monday as I was sitting in my room getting ready for exams during my planning time, Ricky Gerber knocked on the door and asked, "Coach, can I talk to you for a few minutes?"

I said, "Sure, Ricky, what's going on," He looked a little shook up and reluctant to talk. I said, "You look like something is bothering you, son. What is it?"

Ricky with big tears in his eyes said, "Coach, I don't know if I'm going to be able to play next season." He went on to explain that Becky, his girlfriend, told him that morning that she was pregnant. Now that's one of those situation that all the classes and all the studying you did in school just doesn't prepare you for. The first thing I said to Ricky was, "Let's just take time out right now and talk to the Lord about this." That suggestion seemed to satisfy him for the moment, and, besides that, I needed all the help I could get in this situation. More importantly, I believe and I was sure Ricky did too, if there was a way to get through this, the Lord was the only way.

After we prayed for a few minutes, I asked Ricky what his plans were. He said he believed Becky and the baby were his responsibility and he was going to get a job for the summer and that maybe he could hold on to it once school started back. In a few weeks after they had talked to their parents, they wanted to get married. I asked him how he thought his mom and dad would react, even though I already knew the answer. He said he knew they loved him and that they had always stood with him no matter what the situation.

That was really good to hear a young person say in those days and times. With so many problems in families today, for a young man to believe in his parents that much was really nice to hear. Rickey said he knew they would be disappointed in the way things happened, but they really cared about Becky and would want him to take responsibility for what had happened.

The thing he seemed to be worried about the most was that he and Becky both planned on going to college and this would really mess that up. That's when I stopped Ricky and said, "That ain't no hill for a climber, son." Sure, it won't be easy, but people can just about do anything if they want to bad enough. The first thing you do is to get with both Becky's and your parents. Tell them how you feel and what you have on your mind. As far as a job, school, and football go, we will find a way to work that out. The main thing to me is that you both are looking at what's best for this baby, and I believe the good Lord will honor that. So let's take care of first things first, Talk to your parents. We've got a whole summer to work on the other things. Now get going and don't forget two things."

Ricky said, "What's that coach."

I said, "I love you and don't forget to pray."

CHAPTER 6

The other obstacle I was talking about happened just one day later. As I was locking up the field house after school, Coach Meyers drove up and got out of his truck. I said," Coach, what are you doing up here this late in the day? You know we don't get paid any overtime," I laughed. When I looked up and saw the look on his face, I knew something was wrong. David then started to tell me that he and his wife were getting a divorce. Now, that may not be such a shock with so many marriages ending that way in this world today, but what you have to understand is how close a group of guys on a coaching staff can get. It's like a family in itself. When you spend as much time as you do with one another, you naturally get to know each other pretty darn well. It's not always that way, but the really good coaching situations are. There's not a better feeling that you can have than to have a group of fellas you depend on regardless of the situation. That's the way our staff was. We didn't have any ego problems. We all had areas we were strong in and others we needed help in, and we all had a strong faith in God. So when Coach began to tell me what was happening it was tough to handle. I didn't really know what to say or what he wanted me to say. I just asked what if anything I could do and to take all the time he needed once school was out. During the summer we were all involved in workouts starting the next week. So I didn't want him concerned about those until he got things worked out. When David got into his truck to leave, I just said to him, "Remember what I always tell the kids, and it ain't no different for us."

He said, "What's that, Coach?"

I said, "Good things happen to good people, and I know the kind of man you are. Keep your head up, and remember we will all be here for you."

CHAPTER 7

The summer just seemed to fly by in no time at all. There's so much to do in preparation for the next season. There are so many things to get done that you better make a list in order not to forget anything. That's what we did as a staff each year before school was out. On the big board in the office we listed all the things that we had to get done during that time, and as each was completed it was crossed out. Everything from practice schedules to painting the locker room floor was included. During that summer there just seemed to be a little extra pep in each step that everyone took. The players came for their required workouts, and many came around just to be together when they didn't have workouts. The coaches were enthusiastic as they completed the many tasks each passing day, and even Touchdown seemed to feel the excitement as he chased the birds out of the water that sprayed out of the sprinkler system.

In late July we had a week of rain which was highly unusual for hot Alabama summers, but it was welcomed by everyone because of the extreme heat. It also chased everyone indoors, away from the normal activities for this time of the year. This included the work involved in preparation for the upcoming football season.

Normally the grass on the playing field and practice field had to be cut on Monday, Wednesday, and Friday so it would be thick and soft. We wanted a good turf, and this maintenance makes the field look so much better. That's important to us; we want our facilities to look good all the time. We may not have the best that money can buy because our budget is rather small, but we can darn well do all we can to make what we do have look the best it possibly can. The rain gave us a little extra time to make repairs inside that needed to be completed as fall practice was getting closer every day.

CHAPTER 8

We decided as a coaching staff to start fall practice in a different way this year. Our budget wouldn't allow us to go off to a fall camp anywhere, so we decided to have our camp right on campus. Mr. Behel, our principal, gave us permission to use the gym and the cafeteria, so we had the players come in on Sunday evening after church time for what we decided to call, "Boot Camp."

To say that "Boot Camp" was a success would be quite an understatement. With the parents help in preparing three meals each day from Monday through Thursday and the business community as small as it was chipping in financially, the spark we needed to jump start the season was provided. My wife and Ms. K, our school cafeteria manager, planned and prepared the meals for camp which allowed the coaching staff to focus on practice each day.

CHAPTER 9

Our plan was to practice three times each day for four days and then finish up with a game type scrimmage on Friday morning before turning the team loose for some rest over the weekend before school started on Monday. Our players brought sleeping bags to sleep in the gym where we had the needed showers and bathrooms. Each night we showed a movie to the team, and lights went out at 9:00 P. M. sharp.

There was not any problem getting the squad in bed because after the work put in each day all of them were ready. We started the day at 5:00 A. M. with a wake up horn. We then went out on a two-mile run including the coaches and Touchdown before returning to the gym for a shower and then on to the cafeteria for a light breakfast. Before we went to breakfast we had clean up and then a quiet time which included one of the coaches leading a devotional. After breakfast, we had our first practice at 8:00 in shorts and helmets. This was a great time to work on special teams without having to get on the ground, still wet with morning dew. Around 9:30 we would end the morning practice, go back to the gym for a quick shower, and then have group meetings with the different position coaches. This was a little difficult since we only have 38 players and several of them played both offense and defense, but it was a problem we could work around. We had lunch at 11:00 after which we gave the players a few minutes to relax before our noon practice that began at 12:30. This was a very physical period with time devoted to fundamentals, especially blocking and tackling as well as conditioning. This practice was tough on the players as a result of heat, but we took precautions and only worked in eight-minute segments before breaking for ice and fluids. Thank goodness for our local sports medicine folks that assisted us with the concerns we had for our players getting too hot. The trainers were instrumental in the success we had. As tough as those practices were on the players, I believe they were vital to our coming together as a team because we had some leaders step forward during the heat. We tried to end the noon practice at 2:00 although we ran a little long a couple of days in order to get our work in. After the practices ended, our players took a quick shower and had a snack prepared by our parents during lunch. We had snacks set up in our gym concession stand for this, and our managers got everything ready. We could not have had the successful camp without our managers. Any coach will testify that a good manager is worth his weight in gold. Fortunately, we had three- Eddie, Wade and our head man Tom. Tom had his hands full that week helping me keep up with the wash. We usually finished up each night after the players went to bed, but we work well together, and he's a lot like me in making sure everything is clean and organized.

Our afternoon practice got started at 5:00 and ended at 6:30.

This practice was devoted to team offense and team defense. We tried to make this period as much like game situations as possible with the numbers we had. Following the afternoon practice, we always had clean up in the field-house with a rotating schedule for sweeping and mopping the floors. Coaches took care of bathroom cleaning, and before we left everything was ready for the next practice. All the practices, cleaning, and going back and forth was supervised by Touchdown. He went everywhere the team did including the two mile run. Once cleanup was done, we had supper as I call it or dinner to some, our movie and then to bed. Five o'clock in the morning comes early when you are working with youngsters that aren't accustomed to getting up that early.

CHAPTER 10

After the players were bedded down on Tuesday night, all of us coaches were spending a little time rehashing the first two days of camp while drinking a Coke in Coach Spangler's office in the gym. We all agreed it had been two good days, and the idea of bringing all the kids in for the week was allowing us the time to work on our new offense which was a big change from our I - formation run- oriented system of the past. While the spread was more passing-game friendly, we can still run our traditionally running plays from our option look as we move players around with motion. Coach Snow commented that the offensive line was picking up our new blocking scheme well but was a little concerned about our lack of depth if we lost a player to an injury. I said, "Knock on wood. Maybe that won't happen."

We should have all knocked on wood because during our noon practice on Wednesday it happened. Franklin Lacy, our strongest most experienced lineman, went down with a knee injury during a tackling drill. Our trainer was there, and the concern showed on his face as he checked Franklin's knee. He told us it wasn't good, and when Franklin returned from the sports medicine clinic later that afternoon on crutches, it was confirmed. He had a torn ACL. As we talked, he looked really down but quickly asked if he worked really hard during rehab could he be back for the first game of the play-offs. I said, "Let's just get the surgery done and get the rehab started, and we will see how it goes." I was really pleased in Franklin's confidence that we would be in the playoffs, but there were a lot of bridges to cross before that happened.

CHAPTER 11

In our practices on Thursday, we spent time finding guys to step up to take Franklin's place on both sides of the ball. Not only was he our starting left tackle on offense which was so important in pass protection, but he was the nose in our 5 – 2 defensive look. At 5' 11" and 230 pounds, he took up space in the middle controlling both A gaps and keeping offensive linemen off our linebackers. We felt we would be okay on offense with Toby Garner, a junior who could step in and do a good job for us there but as Coach Snow said, we didn't have anyone who could do what Franklin did on defense.

On Thursday, the last full day of "boot camp," we finished up our morning practice talking to our players about stepping up when someone gets hurt as good teams do. We used Franklin's injury to help our players to understand that was why it's important to be ready when your time comes. About the time all our players came together to lift our helmets upward and in unison shout "Team" as we did to end each practice, Mr. Behel, our principal, walked up with two youngsters and an older gentleman.

Mr. Behel said, "Coach this is Howard Jacobs. He is the new

pastor at the Methodist Church. These are his two grandsons, Harrison and Mickey." He went on to say that the two boys were transferring from Benton High School close to Macon, Georgia. "Harrison is a junior and Mickey is a freshman. They want to play football. I told Mr. Jacobs that you would be glad to have two more players."

I thanked Mr. Behel, and he headed back to his office. I asked Mr. Jacob's and his grandsons to walk with me to the gym. I explained to them about what we're doing in camp and that we would be finishing up this afternoon. I further explained that we would have a scrimmage the next morning and would be glad to have them join us. As we talked, I asked Harrison and Mickey about their football team at Benton. I learned Harrison had played both ways for Benton as a tackle while Mickey had been a tailback on their junior high team. Benton had been 5 – 5 the year before with several players returning for this season. I told both youngsters we would be glad to have them join our Eagles team and that we would get them suited up for practice as soon as we finished lunch. I explained about the paper work I needed for eligibility purposes, and they had brought everything with them.

Mr. Jacobs said," The boys would like to get stated practicing today if it would be okay."

I said, "Great, we can get you ready for this afternoon's practice so you can see what we are doing." I looked up when the two boys weren't looking and mouthed, "Thank you Lord".

Harrison was around 6' and maybe 220. I was thinking, could he play nose. He looks big enough and strong enough as well. About that time Lanny and Ricky walked up, and I introduced them to our new players. I told them they would be joining us for lunch, and they began to talk with each other as Mr. Jacobs and I talked about their move to Piney Grove. He told me that the boys had lost their mom and dad in a car accident right after school let out for the summer. He said it had been tough on all the family, but that with the support of friends, prayer, and their faith in God, things were getting better day by day. Mr. Jacobs said he believed it was God's will that their family had moved to Piney Grove and that it would be a new start for his grandsons. I told him we would be praying for his family and that we would take care of his grandsons.

CHAPTER 12

After our afternoon practice on Thursday which seemed like it had been the hottest day of the summer and for sure the most humid of our week of "boot camp," we had a surprise for our team. A couple of the players' dads had arranged to get watermelons from a local farmer, and we had an old fashion watermelon cutting right in front of the field-house. The coaches cut the watermelons in fourths, and I don't believe I have ever seen as much watermelon eaten at one time in my life.

Afterwards, the players thanked Rickey's and Tim's dad, they got all the leftover watermelon rinds up from our surprise, and left to shower in the gym get a little rest before our evening meal. In the meantime the coaching staff had some planning to do before our scrimmage the next morning. We had to divide our players into two squads and decide how to run our scrimmage. There was one thing we had to do: make sure our week ended on a positive note. After the scrimmage the players would be off until practice time on Monday, our first day of school. We wanted a real buzz on campus Monday about our upcoming season, and the opening game was just three weeks away.

CHAPTER 13

Just as we reached the steps of the gym after that Thursday practice, a really pretty young lady drove up in front of the gym. I noticed Coach Meyers had a big smile on his face. He said, "Guys, I want y'all to meet Sara Daugherty; she's a friend of mine".

We all said hello and went on into the gym as they continued to talk by Sara's car. When Coach Meyers came into the gym office, he had another smile on his face. He knew he was about to catch a lot of grief from all of us.

Coach Snow started it off, "What about it, coach? You've been holding out on us, huh!"

Then Coach Barnes chipped in, "Coach, what's the story? How did you rate her?"

I followed up their remarks by saying, "I have always said you can't keep a good man down, but that girl is as pretty as a speckled pup. Tell us about her."

He said, "They had met of all places at the grocery store on the cereal aisle."

Barry responded with, "That just happens on television."

He said, "They had been seeing each other for a couple of weeks and had a good time together."

Coach Snow again spoke up and said, "Seeing each other-you mean dating" and we all laughed.

I went on to tell them that was the second piece of good news I had that day. Earlier, Rickey had told me that he and Becky were getting married the next Friday and asked me about the coaches coming to the ceremony. He said it was going to be a small wedding in his grandmother's back yard, but he would like for us to be there if we could. I told him that I believed I could speak for all of us and we would be there. Ricky went on to tell me that they were going to live with his mom and dad. He said they had been great about everything, and his mom was decorating her sewing room for a little nursery. I told him that didn't surprise me. Your mom and dad are the best parents any young man could ask for. I told the coaches that I wish all our players had parents like his.

CHAPTER 14

O nce we had the team in bed for the night, all the coaches met in Coach Spangler's office again in order to divide our players for the morning intrasquad game. We had had a great week and our goal was really two fold. One was to see how our team responded to a game-type situation in our new offense, and the other was to make sure all the players left for the weekend fired up and ready for practice on Monday. I had contacted our local officials association, and they had agreed to send a crew out the next morning to work the game. We modified the scoring for the scrimmage somewhat since the squad was split. We had tried our best to make it equal, but in an intrasquad game that was nearly impossible. In addition to the regular ways to score, we decided to give 3 points each time the offense had two or more consecutive first downs and 3 points to the defense when they stopped the offense from getting a first down on any possession. We had really emphasized the importance of being able to drive the football offensively all week and at the same time stressed to our defense the importance of not allowing big plays.

CHAPTER 15

T he next morning we allowed the guys to sleep later than usual as wake up was at 7:00. After showers we had a special breakfast with biscuits and chocolate gravy. Following breakfast we met with the team for a short time in order for each coach to say a few words about camp and to explain how the team was split for the scrimmage.

Each coach took his turn talking about our week's work and the progress we had made. I could not have written script for them that would have been better. Coach Barnes talked about our improvement in the weight room and how it had a huge carryover to spring and right on through "Boot Camp." Coach Snow praised the offensive linemen and their focus on adapting to the new blocking scheme we had put in. He went on to say a few words about our young kids as well as how our more experienced guys had gone out of their way to help to push and encourage the younger players to the point that some would be challenging for playing time. This demonstrated the unselfish attitude that had developed during boot camp. Coach Meyers spoke next, talking to the team about how excited he was about the upcoming season and how much fun and enjoyment he had during the week. He said he could feel a bond between all the players and coaches that he had not experienced before which would be a positive factor during the season.

I followed their remarks by saying a few words about how proud I was of the attitude and commitment that was responsible for the progress we had made. "What's most important," I told the players, "is that you never forget how blessed we are to be part of a game that gives us all the opportunity to be better, not just in football, but better and more prepared for what's ahead. One day football or sports of any type will be over as we are part of now, but we still have to be winners in order to have a quality life when we take care of our families as we go about looking for that place the good Lord wants us to be. We can only do that if we do everything we do to the best of our ability and never be satisfied with anything less. This will allow us to be winners regardless of what the scoreboard says."

CHAPTER 16

The intrasquad game brought an end to our week together and laid the groundwork for what we all hoped would be a special season, a season in which each Friday night we competed to our potential after a good week of preparation. If we do that, I told our squad so many times, everything else will take care of itself.

The week in camp was capped off with many bright spots in the scrimmage and had everyone enthused going into the last weekend before school started. One of the highlights was the passing and catching of Lanny alone with our receivers. Everything was clicking during the game, and even the officials commented about the intensity of the game. One of the older officials in the crew that called the scrimmage said it made him look forward to the season getting started.

Officials are such a critical part of the game. Regardless of what level of play they are officiating, the way they approach the game, their hustle, and the way they carry themselves adds to the game. A good crew that cares about the game and the kids makes all the difference in the way it's played. Officials never should believe they are the show, but they are certainly part of it.

CHAPTER 17

Following Friday's morning scrimmage, we hustled the players home. We had already cleaned up the gym after breakfast, so it was just a matter of squaring away things around the fieldhouse, helping Tom get the wash in, and heading home. We all looked forward to the weekend after an enjoyable, but tough camp.

My wife and boys were packed and waiting when I arrived home. We had already planned on this last weekend of summer vacation that we would take a short trip. Our boys loved the zoo, so we hit the road to Memphis. The part of the trip they liked the most was staying in a motel which was big for them. They enjoyed the zoo, but I believe the swimming pool at the motel along with the breakfast buffet at Shoney's was just as much fun for them. A coach's wife and kids put up with a great deal when dad is gone much of the time, so this trip was important for us. I don't believe a coach can enjoy his job and do it well without a wife that is his best friend. He may have the best coaching staff possible, but his most important assistant had better be his wife. And when he gets the opportunity, he better look for opportunities to show her how important she is to him, the family, and the team. If there is to be real success, it needs to be done together. That doesn't always translate into winning games. It means making a difference in the lives of young folks you've been entrusted with in the important years that can make a huge difference in the adults they become.

CHAPTER 18

D riving back from Memphis late Saturday night, the boys were all asleep in the car as I talked to Elaine about school starting and the upcoming season. She said that she could tell a great difference in the attitude and energy all the players had during camp the previous week. She went on to remind me as she had many times during our years together that I needed to remember that I could only do so much. She said, "It's up to the players as to what kind of season we have." I was reminded as we talked that's what a good assistant does; they keep you grounded, reminding you often to just work hard, do all you can in preparation, and then leave it up to the team. My assistant coach is the best. She knows how to pick me up when I'm down and hold me accountable when I get off track. She also reminds me to model what I tell our players regularly. "Do everything you can to be the best, then there are no regrets, and you are always a winner."

Before we went home, I had to go by the field house to check on Touchdown, He stays in the field house; that's home to him. We had a cut out in one of our side doors that allowed him to go in and out as he pleased. He loved it in there. I had asked Coach

Meyers to check on him for me on Saturday. When we got there, he was glad to see us. The boys had to get out for a few minutes to play with him while I got a few things from my desk. Elaine went into the field house with me making the comment, "Sure does smell better in here.

"I said, "Must be the mistifier we have in here to clean and sanitize the air."

"I wonder whose idea that was," she laughed. It was hers.

I told the boys to tell Touchdown bye because we had to go home. I had a little planning to do, and they had to get in bed. Sunday school was in the morning, and it was late.

Sunday after church and lunch I went to the field house for some time to gather my thoughts on Monday's practice schedule. Touchdown was glad to spend the afternoon lying on the floor by my desk. The times I sat at my desk and work on the field were our special times together. He really enjoyed that time, but not any more than I did.

CHAPTER 19

Monday's practice was the first of a three-week run to the first Friday night on the season. Heck! That's an exciting night. There is not anything any better than preparing for the first game of the season with the build up, the anticipation as well as the hard work culminating in seeing the look on a group of youngsters' and coaches' faces as those last few minutes tick off the clock leading up to kick-off. That feeling is hard to describe; I just know it's special. Maybe the reason lies in the fact that on that opening night of the season every team is undefeated and it points to the importance of playing the game. It's all about putting everything you have into something with it all about to be put on display.

Even though we had camp as a way of jump starting pre-season practice, Monday's practice was a big day since school was starting and everyone would be on a regular routine. The best part about school being in session is that we have our players in a more controlled situation. We are blessed in that we don't have many distractions, but as small as we are, there are things that can disrupt our players' focus and discipline at times. We try our best to emphasize those areas over and over to our guys, but we can't forget that we are working with teenagers. Football has to be fun for them, and we are fortunate to have a group of kids who have bought in to our beliefs and what we strive to do. We don't ever want to walk off the field not knowing that we gave everything we had to the best of our ability. If we give our all, if we do all the things necessary to be successful both on and off the field, it won't matter what the scoreboard says.

CHAPTER 20

I didn't sleep much Sunday night. There was so much going on in my mind that I couldn't rest. As usual when the first day of school comes around, I intended to be early. I got up at 4:00 as my regular routine began. I made coffee, checked the weather forecast, had my quiet time, went for a jog, showered, kissed Elaine and left to begin the day.

The first day of school was always a little hectic with new schedules, a few new teachers, and several new students. As I was standing in the hall doing my assigned morning duity, Harrison and Mickey Jacobs walked by with big smiles on their faces. It seemed they had adjusted to their new surroundings pretty well. I noticed Harrison had already made the acquaintance of Misty Forrester, one of our varsity cheerleaders.

My health classes went well that first day. I taught health for three periods in the morning, supervised the lunch periods, had planning during sixth period, and then seventh period athletics. That schedule worked well for me in that it gave me a period to get ready for practice each day since we had most of our players for the last period. As a result of scheduling, there were always a few players we did not have, but that gave us the opportunity to work on special teams each day, which was a real benefit to our kicking game. We also used a few minutes each day for our two-minute drill and our goal-line offense.

CHAPTER 21

The three week stretch to that first Friday night really began to drag during the last week. Coaches and players were ready to see another colored jersey as the players were tired of hitting each other; they wanted to hit someone else. I kept reminding them to stay focused. When players get tired and a little frustrated, the necessary character is built to work through the tough times that come to each of us as individuals and as a team as well. But despite everything we threw at them, this group kept on grinding and continued to work hard. All of us coaches began to ask each other when was the storm going to come. It never did. We got to that last practice before game day without any more major injuries or pitfalls as the Lord continued to bless us.

Friday morning arrived finally and it was game day. There was so much excitement on campus that morning I began to wonder if Mr. Behel was going to be able to get the students to class when the bell rang. He finally got on the intercom and announced to the students that we had to have class for a little while. He was so supportive of our team and the students in everything they did. All the kids loved and respected him. Our players had decided that they wanted to wear slacks, dress shirts, and ties for our first game day of the year, and the coaches did the same. The players usually wore game jerseys and the coaches dressed in slacks and polo shirts, but again this group is special. They also decided to meet in the hall intersection after each class at which time one of the seniors would say a few words about the game. When they did that after the first period of the day, a few other students gathered around the team. By the end of third period, word had spread, and most of the students were joining in.

That afternoon we had a great pep rally led by the band and cheerleaders. Many of the parents attended the pep rally as well. Near the end of the pep rally it was tradition that I announce our captains who spoke to our student body, encouraging them to get out and support the team at the game. The captains that first week were Ricky Gerber and Lanny Hubbard. Both had been the driving force behind our successful pre-season. When Ricky took the microphone, the student body exploded. He had gained the respect of the students and everyone in the community as a result of the way he had stepped up as a young man and had become an example in accepting the challenge of being a father, playing football, staying in school, and working a part-time job. Following Ricky, I spoke to the students and parents thanking them for their support and telling them how important it was for our team.

Following the pep rally, the players reported to the cafeteria for a light pre-game meal prepared by Ms. K and then to the field house where they checked their equipment for the game. We had already done the same thing the day before following our Thursday walk through, but we always wanted to make sure everything was in order. Tom and his crew had already packed the extra equipment we took on the road along with our medical bag for the short trip down highway 72 to "Bears Stadium," where in just a little over three hours we would kick off the season against our arch rival, the Farmington Bears. The Bears football program was steeped in tradition. They had won the 2-A State Championship two years earlier and had a solid program led by Coach Jon May, who had been their head coach for the past twelve years. It was kind of unusual that we play our biggest rival in the first game of the season, but it was a great money game for both schools. Schools our size had to really budget well to have the funds to finance our programs in the way we want to. We made sure our players had everything they needed to be safe and look good, too. We take a great deal of pride in putting on our royal blue, white, and silver uniforms.

After the equipment was checked and everything was ready for our bus ride, we had last minute position meetings with our offense, defense, and special teams going over everything from A to Z. We even reviewed how we were going to line up and go through our pre-game warm up. There was nothing left to chance.

When the clock reached 5:00, we called all our players together for a few last-minute remarks prior to loading the buses for the trip to Farmington. I reminded the players about their hard work in the off season, through spring, during the summer, during boot camp, and fall practice. I said, "Something very special started back in November, and tonight we are starting down a road that will be special to us for the rest of our lives."

It took about 30 minutes for the short ride to the stadium.

The players were really quiet during the trip. As I looked around, none of them were dozing off as was the norm for bus rides. There was an intense look on the face of each player.

We had emphasized over and over about the importance of focusing on each play, playing it to our best ability, moving on the next play, and doing the same thing again. From the looks in their eyes, I believe the time we spent on that process was time used well.

When we pulled up to the fieldhouse, not a player said a word. Players walked over to our equipment truck that Coach Snow had driven down, picked up their gear, walked in, and put it in their lockers. We then walked to the other end of the field and back as we usually did before each game. Coach Meyers was walking next to me, and the players were still not talking as we walked. I said to Coach, "This is a little hard to believe."

He said, "what, coach?"

I said, "How quiet they are."

He said, "Quiet before the storm."

I said, "That's right, We are about to send a storm warning to every team on our schedule, by golly."

CHAPTER 22

The storm started on the kick off. What was amazing is that it was two sophomores on our squad that sounded the alert. Perry Crockett kicked off, and the ball carried to the three yard line. The kick had good hang time. We got our coverage team down the field in their correct lanes, and then it happened. Drayden Sutter was the other sophomore who had lined up as what we call the cannon position, the outside player on the kicking team who has the responsibility to get to the return man as fast as possible in order to make the tackle or at least get a piece of him so others can close him out. Drayden did more than that; he arrived about the time the ball did, which is kind of unusual on a kick off and delivered a snot knocker on the return man. A snot knocker is when a player is hit so hard that snot comes out of his nose. From that point on, the tone was set. It was one of those nights where everything clicked. Following the hit Drayden delivered, we held the Bears to a three and out, and they punted. We gathered in the punt after a fair catch and started our first possession on our 36 yard line. On our first play we ran a bootleg off our toss sweep action with Ricky Gerber running a deep drag route across the middle after showing a block on the Bears' linebacker. Lanny got on the edge after faking the toss and found Ricky wide open about 15 yards down the field. Lanny lofted the ball right into his hands and he was off to the end zone. He made their safety miss at about the 12 yard line and went into score. From that point the route was on, which didn't happen often to Farmington. The final score was 31 – 6, and that was just the beginning.

CHAPTER 23

Following the season-opening victory over our most bitter rival, our season got better and better. The following week we defeated our first area opponent, Rockwood, in a nail-biting last second win 21 – 20. The Trojans were up 20 – 14 with just over 2 minutes on the clock, and we drove the ball 65 yards to score with 14 left in the game. The big play in the drive was a throwback pass from our tailback Tim Burger to Lanny that covered 38 yards. On the play Lanny tossed the ball on a sweep look, which is one of our best plays, but instead of running the ball, he pulled up after taking the pitch and laid the ball into Lanny's outstretched hands streaking down the opposite side line. We ran Lanny down the short side of the field making it a more difficult pass for Tim. We not only faked the toss sweep, but also faked the halfback pass to the strong side, having both our split and slot receivers fake blocking down and then running deep routes through the secondary bringing the Trojans' defense's attention away from Lanny. The most impressive element about the last second win was that in the past years more often than not we usually came up short in close games.

The kids were so excited after that win along with everyone else from our school and community that we had to ask the fans to head on home so we could all get home to our families as well. Mr. Behel took care of the situation in a respectful manner as he always did. He got on the P.A. and said. "Folks we really thank you for the great support, but it's getting late. The Trojans have left the building so be careful on your way home."

I couldn't wait to hug my wife and boys after the game. There had been so many nights when the results were the opposite. Touchdown was even jumping up and down, he got more pats on the head than we as coaches got handshakes. Two straight victories to start the season, we are topping cotton as the "ole timer" would say.

CHAPTER 24

In opening the season with back-to-back victories, our players began to experience unknown ground for Eagles football. It had been three seasons since we had won more than two games and five since we had even a four-win year Excitement was running high on campus, in the community, and even the <u>Daily Courier</u>, our local newspaper who had run an article about the way we had opened the season. But in the article, the writer made the statement that this week's opponent would end the surprise beginning to our season as we faced the defending area champion, the Newton Tigers. The Tigers were also 2 – 0, and they had captured their area title three years in a row. In the year before, Newton had advanced to the simi-finals of the state playoffs. Ordinarily it might have been a little hard to keep our players from thinking too much of themselves, but the article helped the coaching staff take care of that. All week long we put emphasis on the fact that it's not how we start the season as much as how we prepare each week to get ready to play our next opponent that will tell the real story of our season. We constantly reminded them to remember what had led to the start we were experiencing and that if we continue to work hard, play each game one at a time, and never give up, then we will always have an opportunity for success.

CHAPTER 25

When Newton's players got off their big chartered buses Friday night I could almost feel our stadium tilt. They looked so big in their solid green uniforms and to a man we were out weighed at most every position on both offense and defense. As we took the field it was quite an experience. Our home stands were completely filled with fans standing on the banks and around the fence. The Newton stands were filled to capacity as well. Mr. Behel passed by as we were leaving the dressing room and said, "Coach, I believe this is the largest crowed we have every had at Piney Grove." He had a big smile on his face which was an indication of two things on his mind. The community had really showed up to support their Eagles and we would be able to pay some bills.

During warm-ups I could tell our players were really fired up by their emotions during our pre-game drills, but that was brought to a fever pitch when Newton's players circled up on our side of the field as warm-ups came to a close pointing their fingers while chanting "not tonight." When we got back to our dressing room we had to settle the team down before we could go over our last few instructions and have our prayer. I said "Men, all that finger pointing that just happened out there is going to be icing on the cake when we grab those Tigers by the tail in just a few minutes." The team about went crazy when I said that and almost took the door down as we went on the field.

The storm that began in our first game against Farmington grew even stronger that night. It began again on the kick off with another snot knocker by Drayden Sutter. We all thought the hit he delivered our first game was really something to behold, but it was nothing compared to the one he delivered on the Newton return man. When Drayden hit their tailback who returned kicks and had been named to the All-State team the previous year, he went one way, Drayden went another, and the ball flew up and was caught in mid air by Harrison Jacobs, who returned it 26 yards for a touchdown.

We stopped the Tigers after the next kick off on a three and out, setting up the next lighting strike. Newton's punter lofted a nice kick that came down to Ricky Gerber on our 32 yard line. He made their sprint man miss, got to the wall we had set up, and went untouched for a 68-yard touchdown run. Tony Peck, our placement kicker, added the extra point, and we were up 14 – 0 with over six minutes left in the first quarter of play.

We kicked off to Newton for the third time in the first quarter, and things got better for us as they fumbled on their second play from scrimmage. We recovered on the Tigers 27-yard line. We ran our bootleg play after the recovery, and Lanny scored, cutting back across the field around the 15 with the help of Toby Garner, who had sprinted down the field to deliver a great block on their linebacker pursuing the ball carrier. We were up 21 – 0 with 1:25 left in the first quarter, and the storm continued. After the first quarter, there was a little calm before the front moved on through, but the final was 42 – 0. Following the game, one of Newton's coaches asked me what we did to get our players to over achieve the way we had. I said, "Coach, I don't know what you are asking. We don't consider anything we do as over achieving. We just look at it as when preparation and hard work meets success."

CHAPTER 26

Following the victory over Newton, history was made at Piney Grove. We went on the road for two weeks and defeated both Adams and Sherwood, followed that with a home win against area foe Taylorsville, and claimed another road win over Parker County. So seven games deep in the season, we were 7 – 0 overall and 3 – 0 in the area, which was a first for our school. Even one of the big newspapers in the state called me to ask about visiting the campus to do an article on the "Gold Dust Twins." That's what the local paper had dubbed Ricky and Lanny. This worried me a little. It wasn't that either player didn't deserve the attention they were receiving because the seasons they had going were tremendous. The passing of Lanny along with Ricky's receiving exploits were amazing. They were putting up some fabulous stats. The worry I had was how all that attention was going to affect our team.

We had emphasized the team first concept all through our off season starting in November, through the spring, during summer workouts, and now as the most successful season we have ever had was progressing. That Monday afternoon following practice, I shared my concerns with Coach Snow, Coach Myers, and Coach Barnes. I said, "Guys we have been successful this year beyond our greatest expectations for three reasons. One, our making God the focal point in everything we say and do. Two, the hard work put forth by our entire squad. And three, the fact that we have all been as one. The focus on the team has not waivered even with our being 7 – 0, but I am just concerned."

Coach Snow responded, "Coach, I agree, but it's hard to take away from what Ricky and Lanny have accomplished. They are both deserving of the attention. This morning Mr. Tate was telling me that Lanny has thrown twelve touchdowns passes, run for three, and only has one interception during the first seven games. That's quite a season. Ricky has 36 receptions, 6 touchdowns on passes from Lanny, along with 2 punt returns for touchdowns."

"I know," I said, "Mr. Tate told me the same thing."

Mr. Tate was one of our math teachers at Piney Grove and did a great job keeping our stats. Coach Meyers then said, "You know we have been emphasizing team first all year long."

Coach Barnes followed, "You can lead a horse to water, but you can't make him drink."

Then I said, "I believe everything will be fine, but let's all pray that God's will is done."

After supper that night as Elaine and I were cleaning the table and washing dishes while the boys got ready for bed, I talked to my most important assistant coach about my concerns. I explained the situation. As usual, she led me in the right direction. She said, "Honey, you said all along these kids are special, so don't doubt them now."

CHAPTER 27

laine was right; I should never have doubted. First thing Tuesday morning, Lanny and Ricky stopped by the hallway where I was standing and asked to talk to me. I kind of knew it was about the story that the writer from the <u>Birmingham Dispatch</u> was coming to do that afternoon. We went into the library and sat down at one of the back tables. .

I said, "What about it fellas?"

Lanny spoke first, "Coach, we don't want to do this interview if it going to be just about us, It's not right."

Ricky then said, "If it can't be about the entire team from the managers to the coaches, to the players, the school, the community, and even Touchdown we don't want to do it."

I said," Wow, you guys make me so proud. I will take care of it, and you can be assured Mel Sample, the writer from the <u>Dispatch,</u> will know exactly how you feel."

When the article came out on Thursday, the day before Friday night's game, it was not titled "The Gold Dust Twins" as Mr. Sample originally had intended. Instead he titled his article, "Humility, I Found It." The first line said, "If you are like me and often wonder where humility went, I found it in Piney Grove, Alabama."

The article in the newspaper was greatly responsible for the next two victories as we defeated Bethel and Oak Grove in our next two outings. We were sitting at 9 – 0 with the Area Championship and the number one seed in the first round of the State Playoffs on the line in our next game against Truman High.

Our team was even more united after what the story said about the unselfish attitude of our team and was instrumental in our playing the two most complete games I had ever been associated with.

CHAPTER 28

The buildup to the Area Championship game against Truman was unbelievable. The excitement for our team, school, and community was exactly what high school football is all about.

It started first thing Monday morning as we began the week with a pep rally organized by our cheerleaders and band at 7:55 just as the students normally reported to class. Mr. Behel made the announcement for everyone to go to the gym where an explosion happened. Ordinarily it's usually hard to get young people motivated that early, but not that week. We had a pep rally of all pep rallies. When Touchdown came prancing in right in the middle of things, our students went wild. He was jumping up and down, and the more he jumped the more they cheered.

That was the first of many special events that week. The players received gifts everyday from the cheerleaders, the teachers provided breakfast on Wednesday for the team, and the local churches went together and provided a great meal and a special motivational speaker to talk to the team in the fellowship hall of the Baptist Church down the road from the school on Thursday evening after practice.

CHAPTER 29

The speaker after dinner Thursday evening was Jed Painter. He was fantastic. He was a former coach who had experienced the joys and sense of accomplishments of having led teams to state championships on two occasions, but what he was most noted for was the Christian values he taught the players he had coached for over twenty years.

Coach Painters message to the team told of a farmer and his three boys. The farmer had worked hard all his life and taught his sons to do the same and to never expect something for nothing. One morning at the breakfast table, the famer told his sons that he was getting older and he wanted to leave them something to help them to get their own start in life. He said, "Boys, there is a treasure buried back there in that pasture land we have let lay fallow for the past few years. All you have to do is to plow it up to get your reward."

The boys got together and came up with a game plan as to how to gain the prize. One of the sons was going to plow up the north end of the field, another the south, and the last son the middle.

They worked for two days from daylight to dark plowing until they finished, but no treasure was to be found. After searching and searching the boys went to their father and explained the problem to him.

He looked at his three tired young men and said, "You have it, you plowed the ground, now plant the corn and the harvest is yours." The boys all looked at their daddy, then at each other, smiled and hugged his neck.

Coach said, "Your Eagles football team is just like the farmer's sons. You plowed the field all during the off season, during the summer, during "boot camp," now you are reaping the harvest. You have worked hard. The crop is almost in. Finish up tomorrow night, and shut the barn door."

CHAPTER 30

By game time Friday night, our stadium was standing room only. They had arrived around 5:30 for the 7:00 kick off. When they got off the buses, there were fans already seated in the bleachers on both sides of the field. The Truman coaching staff and players were much like us, excited and fired up.

Their season mirrored ours to an extent in that we were both having seasons that had not been the norm for our programs as wins and losses go. We stood at 9 – 0 while they had one loss coming in with an 8 – 1 mark.

Their head coach, Mark Wilson, was a good friend, and our coaches got along really great. I told Coach Snow on the way to the game that it was going to be a shame for either team to lose after both struggling through some tough years. I felt like it would be a great game and that one of us would make one more big play than the other to win it.

Truman did something no other team had done all year long to us. They scored two first-quarter touchdowns, and we were down 14 – 0 early. One of the scores came on an interception as

Lanny's pass sailed a little high right into the hands of their safety. He returned it 85 yards for their second score.

We had been knocking on their door and had moved the ball near the 15 yard line with a first down when the pass was picked off. We had been having success running our sweep with Tim Burger picking up big chunks of yardage when I decided to throw the ball. I felt like we needed to keep them honest by throwing on first down.

In the second quarter we moved the ball down the field again with our running game. Even though we were spreading them out, our toss sweep continued to work well as our pulling guards and wide receivers were making great blocks.

On second down and two at their 24, we ran our inside trap play off our toss sweep fake with Landon Hooks, our little flanker, carrying the ball. He had gone in motion, geared down just outside our tight end, and came back inside off of Bart Jones, our right guard's trap block. The hole burst wide open, and he ran the ball to the 6-yard line where he was hit by Truman's safety and cornerback jarring the ball loose. Truman recovered and killed the last few seconds of the half taking a 14 – 0 lead into the locker room.

CHAPTER 31

During halftime as usual, Tom and his crew took care of the players' needs. They had soft drinks ready for them, towels to wipe their sweat. and extra hardware to repair equipment if needed. Our sports medicine guys also were available for any injuries we might have. Thankfully, there weren't any major problems to deal with.

While that was going on during those few minutes, Coach Snow, Coach Meyers, Coach Barnes, and I along with Coach Spangler, who worked in the press box, got our heads together to discuss any adjustments for the second half. We talked about how well we had been able to run the ball and how well we had defended the run which are usually key factors in being successful in most football games.

But, as Coach Barnes said. "Those dang turnovers killed us."

I finally said, "Men, we decided to put the spread in during the off season because we believed we have the kids with the skills to pass the ball more. We worked on it during the spring and in fall camp, and we still had that same confidence. Our players believe in it too, so we are about to find out if we can put it in the air successfully against a really good team and if they can defend it when we throw the kitchen sick at them."

We told all the players to get a knee and to listen up. I said, "Guys, you played hard that first half, but we made a few mistakes. We had a couple of fumbles, and I made a couple of calls I'd like to have back. Defensive players keep doing what you did the first half. Play with that same intensity, read your keys, and the offense is about to crank up the storm again. We are going to throw the ball more this half, so take care of your responsibilities. Let's pass block like we have all season, run good routes, pick up any blitzes, and Lanny will put the ball on our receivers." And he did.

CHAPTER 32

Truman kicked off to start the half, and the ball bounced into the end zone. We started at the 20-yard line and marched the ball 80 yards for a touchdown on 14 plays taking nearly nine minutes off the clock.

Lanny completed 7 of 8 passes, and Tim had a nice 12-yard gain on a toss sweep that picked up a first down on third and five. Ricky caught the touchdown pass on fade route to the corner of the end zone.

It was 14 – 7 with 6:12 left in the third.

Truman picked up two first downs on their next possession, but we stuffed them on third and two for a 3-yard loss after that forcing a punt with a little over one minute left in the third quarter.

Ricky fielded Truman's punt on our 24-yard line, made their sprint man miss, and gained eight more yards to the 32.

We started the drive 68 yards from pay dirt, and Truman made us earn every one of them in order to tie the game.

It was another 14-play drive, and this one took nearly eight minutes off the clock. Lanny was on target again hitting slant and stop routes seven times enroute to the score. We connected on three third downs and one fourth down with Tim scoring on a wheel route as he motioned out of the backfield. On the fourth down play we needed one yard, so we called time out to talk about the play we wanted to run.

During the timeout Franklin Lacy patted me on the shoulder and said, "Coach, put me in at that left guard and have Lanny run right behind me on keeper. I'll get us that yard." Franklin had been rehabbing his knee, and this was his first game to dress since his injury.

I looked at Franklin and said, "Okay, son, it's you and Lanny.

He got us the yard with two more to spare. First down.

We made the Generals punt again on their next possession after they picked up one first down. The clock was down to 5:02 with the score still knotted up at 14 all.

After their punt, we took over at our own 42, which was 58 yards away from a perfect 10 – 0 season and the playoffs.

On the first play, we ran our inside trap again, and this time Landon wrapped both arms around the ball, gaining 14 yards for another first down. We ran a slant to Ricky next for 12 yards moving the ball down to the 32 yard line with 3:45 left on the clock.

Truman stopped us on the next two snaps for short gain, making it third and seven with 2:06 left.

We called our last time out and decided to run our toss again for the first down. We ran it for what must have been the twentieth time that night with Tim gaining 9 yards and another first down at the 21.

The referee wound the clock into motion with 1:46 left. On

the next play, we ran another slant to Ricky, but we got only 5 yards and the clock was moving. We had to spike the ball with only 54 seconds left.

I looked over at Coach Meyers and said, "We are about to win this game on the best play in football."

I called "18 bootleg," Lanny faked the toss to Joey, put the ball on his hip, ran the naked boot, and lofted the ball to Ricky running across the middle toward the pylon.

Ricky caught the pass in the corner of the end zone. After successfully kicking the PAT, the score stood at 21 – 14 with only 28 seconds left on the clock.

I told Coach Barnes, who was in charge of our kicking game, to kick the ball deep.

Our coverage had been good all season; in fact it had been a huge part of our success. There was no reason to doubt it now. We didn't want to squib kick which might result in their having the ball around midfield. That would allow for a deep route by a receiver that might result in a reception or possibly an interference call.

We covered the kick well with the two Harrison brothers combining for the stop on Truman's 24-yard line.

Coach Snow called our defense together and said, "Guys, this is it. One stop and we will be sitting at 10 – 0, area champs with the top seed going into the state playoffs." We have worked too hard to let this get away. "I said, "holding out my open hand. It's just like this, we have this palm of our hand. Go out there and close the *deal," as I closed my hand.*

Truman did just as we expected; they lined up in trips running all three receivers deep. Their QB threw the ball as far as he could. It didn't matter. The ball was knocked down at about our 35 by Gary Pierce, our strong safety.

The celebration began.

After shaking hands our players, all of them to a man along with the coaching staff and the managers, went up into the stands to join in with all our fans as our band played the fight song.

And as the celebration continued, someone called out, "Look whose coming across the field." It was Touchdown running as hard as he could to join in the fun.

My boys had let him out of our equipment room where he stayed during home games, and he wanted in on the action. He never even stopped to check out the hamburger and hot dog wrappers as he ran up the steps and jumped in my arms.

CHAPTER 33

O ur coaching staff and players met as usual on Saturday morning at 9:00 to look at our game film and go over any mistakes we had made the night before. That morning it was hard to dwell on mistakes as a result of what we had accomplished during the season. Knowing where we had been and how hard everyone had worked to get where we had come to was as good as it could get for a team, especially at a school and in a community that had never experienced anything like it before.

Once the players, left we sat down to look at game films of our first opponent in the playoffs. Since we were the top seeded team as result of our 4 – 0 record in the area, we would meet the number two seeded team in the area our State Athletic Association had us scheduled to play, in this case, it happened to be a rematch with the Newton Tigers.

Since we had met Newton earlier in the season, they had lost twice more following their loss to us, but had closed out the season at 7 – 3 and a second place finish in their area.

We were looking at game film to find tendencies on the part of the Tigers both offensively and defensively as well as to check for any major changes Newton had made during the latter half of the season. I reminded our staff of what their assistant coach had said after our first meeting.

I said, "Fellas do y'all remember what Coach Tank said after the first game we played?"

Coach Meyers responded, "Yea, about our players performing over their heads."

Coach Snow then said, "That rubs me a little the wrong way."

I said, "Me, too, but what we are about to do is to not only play above our heads, we're going to play out of our mind. This time Newton's going to see us do some things totally unexpected from a Piney Grove team.

Coach Barnes asked, "Coach what's the plan?"

In the next two hours we put together a game plan that not only included our spread game featuring our short quick passing game, our sweep plays, and our bootlegs, but we added more play action vertical passes than we had ever attempted. We also added a couple of trick plays on offense that we had not used during the season along with a throw back on the kickoff that I had not seen since I had played years before.

Our mind-boggling plans did not stop on the offensive side of the ball. We decided to blitz on most every defensive call, which was really a contrast to our usual bend, but not break conservative approach on defense. We even decided to onside kick the first time we had to kick off in the game and to fake a punt the first opportunity we had. We were about to break many of the tendencies Newton would expect after viewing films of our games.

CHAPTER 34

Following Monday afternoon's practice, we called the players in to take a knee before going in for the day. We discussed practice that day and what we were going to do on Tuesday. As usual, we asked the team if anyone had a question or anything on their mind.

I had no more got the words out of my mouth when Tim Burger said, "Coach, I don't mean to be disrespectful, but are you sick?"

I said, "No, Tim, why do you ask?"

He said, "Coach, the changes we put in today are about as far from what I would expect from our coaching staff than anything I could ever imagine." When he said that, the entire team started agreeing.

I said, "Guys let me explain a few things. That saying about you can't teach an old dog new tricks is completely untrue. We have been to a trainer and come back like a litter of puppies, ready to try anything."

The players exploded with laughter when I said that.

Practice went well that week. On Thursday we had another

surprise. As we were finishing up Mr. Behel walked up and said, "Coach, when you get finished have everyone go in and take a seat in the locker room. I have something I want to share with them. It's a little cold to stand out here."

When all the players had sat down, Mr. Behel began. "Men," he said, "this has been a great season for you, our school, and our community. The success you have had on the field and the way you have carried yourselves off the field has brought a great deal of pride to all of us involved. The leadership provided by the coaches and you players as well has been something I will always be proud of. You have displayed humility and character in everything you have done this year, and all the people in this area are well aware of it. But now people all over our state and in the southeast are going to have an opportunity to see it. This week's game with Newton has been chosen to be the Tri – States Sports Networks high school game of the week."

Coaches, players and managers sat there with our mouths open when he finished talking. It was hard for us to believe that the Piney Grove Eagles were going to be on television.

Just as Mr. Behel was finishing his announcement that had surprised us all, Touchdown came through his opening in the door, stood in the middle of the dressing room floor and wagged his tail as if to say, "I am not staying in the equipment room this Friday night."

CHAPTER 35

The school and community was buzzing with excitement after Mr. Behel's announcement, but not anything like it was when the three big Tri – State Sports trucks pulled into our parking lot first thing Friday morning.

Mr. Behel was prepared as usual. He had informed our county maintence department and the utility department as to our needs for the broadcast. It was being taken care of.

By game time Friday night our stadium was a sight to see. It looked like an SEC game was about to be played.

Ordinarily we would have been worried about how this would affect our players, but as we already knew, this team had something special.

By game time it was business as usual. Everything was ready; our players were fired up and had done a great job of blocking out all of the distractions.

We won the toss and chose to defer until the second half. As we lined up to kick off, all our eyes were on how they lined up to receive. Just as we had hoped, they were prepared for a regular kick.

When Perry Crockett kicked the ball, he hit it near the top, which made the ball take a big hop just as it reached the first Newton player.

The ball went off his hands, and Drayden Sutter made another big play, recovering the ball at Newton's 42-yard line.

We scored in three plays. The touchdown came when Lanny faked the hand off to Tim Burger, took a step back, and hit Ricky Gerber in full stride, running a post route past their safety that had bit on the fake.

Following the touchdown, we had another surprise for the Tigers. When the ball was snapped to Ricky, who was the holder on all our placements, he caught the ball, rolled to his right, and threw a perfect pass to Mickey Harrison in the back of the end zone for a two-point conversion.

After that, it seemed like Newton could not do anything right.

We scored on the faked punt we had planned right before the half to make the score 22 – 0 and on the throwback on the kickoff to start the third stanza.

On that play Lanny was deep to return the kick. When he caught the ball, he headed up the right sideline just like a regular kick return. But, when he got about 5 yards from their first player in coverage, he stopped and planted, throwing a backwards pass across the field to Tim, who caught the ball, got a block from Toby Garner, and scored untouched.

It was 29 – 0 and we tacked on another score early in the fourth quarter to win our first ever playoff game 36 – 0.

We learned later that we would face the Parrish Mustangs in the second round of the playoffs. They were 11 – 0 just like us and were ranked number one in the state. The game would be played on the Mustangs, home turf.

CHAPTER 36

The game was billed to be the headline game of the state football playoffs, but it didn't turn out that way. It was a cold rainy night with a few snow flurries mixed in, creating a slick field and bad footing for both teams. Thank goodness for our running game because passing was near impossible with the cold and the slick ball.

Parrish was a full-scale spread option team that relied greatly on misdirection and their passing game. This worked to our favor as we reverted back to our three-yards-and-cloud-of-dust attack. On that night, it became three yards and mud in the face.

We won the game 13 – 6 and followed that up with a 20 – 14 win the next week on the road at Millersburg in what was another wet night. After thirteen games we were undefeated as we continued to make history in Piney Grove, Alabama.

Following our semi-final victory, we met with the team on Saturday morning to look at the film of our victory over Millersburg. It wasn't pretty. That was no surprise considering the conditions we had played in for the second week in a row.

We didn't have any game film of our opponent in the finals,

but we would be attending a meeting later in the day at our state office to swap tapes and get all the information related to the event. The only thing we knew was that our opponent would be the Collier Wolves a tradition rich program from south Alabama that was a regular in the playoffs having won State Championships on three different occasions.

We scheduled a team meeting after church on Sunday. We would have the details then for everyone concerned so plans could be made for the biggest athletic event ever to take place involving Piney Grove sports.

CHAPTER 37

All the teams taking part in the state football playoffs were required to send a representative to the meeting at the state office Saturday afternoon at 4:00. During the meeting we received the instructions needed for the game on Friday.

We learned the game would be played on a neutral site at Municipal Stadium in Norton, Alabama, located near Birmingham. Our coaching staff was not familiar with the stadium, but other coaches that attended the meeting said the city and the facility was a great place to play the game.

We met with Collier's coaches at the meeting to exchange tape and to get acquainted. Their head coach and his assistants were really nice. In many situations when a program had the success Collier had, there was the possibility of their having an air about them of "just who do you think you are playing an established program like ours?"

It was not that way at all with Coach Yancey and his staff. He said, "Coach" let me know if I can help in any way this week. I know this is your first time in the finals, and I sure want to help it be a good experience for y'all."

I replied, "Coach, that's the nicest thing I've heard during the playoffs. I hope our program can be like the one you have built someday."

He smiled in return and said, "I believe you have it going in the right direction."

On Sunday afternoon there was good and bad news. The good was the weather. After two weeks of cold, wet, and sometimes snowy weather, the sun was out. Even though the cold was still with us, sunshine was a welcomed change. The forecast for Friday's championship game was for more of the same.

The bad was the number of players we had sick. Several had coughs, many were congested, and a few had temperatures. The two hardest hit were Ricky Gerber and Tim Burger. Both had fever and really needed to be home in the bed.

I talked to our squad about the details of our trip to the game on Friday, our practice schedule for the week, and a little snap shot of what to expect from the Wolves on offense and defense.

I said, "Guys, we will spend the afternoon looking at film and putting a game plan together. When we turn you lose in a few minutes, go home, rest, and enjoy what we have accomplished. You fellas that are under the weather, go to bed, drink plenty of fluids and eat something even though you may not feel like it. You have to keep your strength and energy level up as much as possible."

I then said, "Everybody in here on a knee. Let's thank God for how He has blessed, us, pray for those not feeling well, ask for guidance, and that we seek His will in our lives."

Once the players left, Coach Meyers said, "It's not good when you have your starting tailback and leading receiver out when we are trying to win the State Championship."

I said, "No, it's not, but we have to prepare for that possibility. I have no doubt those two young men will suit up for the game. What I don't know is how much, if any, they will be able to play. We have to get Mickey ready at tailback, and we will move Landon to Ricky's position some this week as well. I know both of those youngsters are not as experienced as Ricky and Tim, but we will get their best effort. No doubt about that."

We began Monday afternoon moving some folks around just in case we had players too sick to play. The number sick had grown to ten, and we were keeping our fingers crossed that more didn't join them. All the players were at practice despite not feeling well. I don't believe wild horses could have kept them away.

Practice was really good on Monday and Tuesday even though we were short handed. Mickey and Landon looked good in their positions, and those sick seemed to be coming around. Excitement around campus and in the community was at a fever pitch as game day grew near. Each day that week, there was an article in the newspaper about the upcoming game as we even had another visit from Mel Sample, the writer from the <u>Dispatch,</u> to do a follow up story on our season.

CHAPTER 38

Tuesday during lunch, Mr. Behel came in and sat down by me. He said, "Coach, several parents have called about the possibility of chartering buses and taking the team on down Thursday afternoon after practice for the game. They indicated that sponsors in the community are willing to pay the expenses. What do you think?"

I thought for a minute and said, "That's really nice that they want to do that, but if it's okay with you I had rather stay with the routine we have followed for thirteen weeks now. I guess I am old fashioned, superstious, or whatever it might be called, but we have our plan laid out, and I believe it will be best if we follow it. If you don't mind explain that to them and ask them to do something for the team after the game. I don't think we need to put the wagon before the horse."

He said, "It's your call. What we have done has worked, so keep it up."

I said, "Thanks Mr. Behel."

Our staff had talked to the team all year long about being ready when our time comes. We had reiterated that again during the week, and our players were once again focused on the task that lay ahead. On Thursday we finished up our walk through with most of the players back to full strength except Ricky and Tim. Both were better, but we intended to start the game with Mickey and Landon. Ricky and Tim had been able to get some reps in on Wednesday, but we could tell they were pushing themselves to go.

CHAPTER 39

We had our pep rally on Friday during third period, ate lunch at noon, and boarded the buses at 1:00 p. m. sharp for the trip to Norton. The journey took about two and a half hours.

As we traveled down the interstate, it looked like a caravan behind us. We couldn't believe how many cars were lined up as we traveled south.

Norton was on the south side of Birmingham. The information we had received about Municipal Stadium being nice was absolutely correct. It looked like a college stadium. When we pulled up, there wereTV cameras everywhere. Our players were as excited as I had ever seen a group of young folks.

Several of our parents had arrived before we got there in order to prepare the team a light meal. All those traveling with us had one huge tail gate party. As I got off the bus, I saw Elaine and my boys standing over by our van. When I looked, I could not believe my eyes, Touchdown was on a leash jumping up and down. I kissed Elaine and said, "This must be a dream."

CHAPTER 40

Touchdown barked, waking me up to see the smiling face of Dr. Stanley standing in the office doorway.

Doc said, "Man, you was dead to the world, but you had a tiny grin on your face.

"I said, "You won't believe the dream I just had."

Doctor Stanley is a professor at our local college and is also involved in the North-Med Sports Medicine Group that supports all the high school football teams in our area. We have been friends since I took a graduate class with him several years ago.

On Friday nights, he is always assigned to cover one of the local football games in order to provide medical support as a licensed trainer on the sidelines. However, regardless of where he is assigned, I can always count on him swinging by our stadium on his way home to check on us.

He said, "I heard on the radio on the way here that y'all lost another close one tonight. After seeing that grin on your face as you were dozing, I thought maybe I heard the score wrong."

I said, "Doc, let me give Elaine a call. Tonight we're going to my house and have a toasted scrambled egg sandwich while I tell you about *The Season That Never Was.*

I picked up the phone and said, "Honey, put on the coffee. "Doc" is coming home with me to eat a bite."

Printed in the United States
By Bookmasters